A Note to Parents and Caregivers:

Read-it! Readers are for children who are just starting on the amazing road to reading. These beautiful books support both the acquisition of reading skills and the love of books.

The RED LEVEL presents familiar topics using common words and repeating sentence patterns.
The BLUE LEVEL presents new ideas using a larger vocabulary and varied sentence structure.
The YELLOW LEVEL presents more challenging ideas, a broad vocabulary, and wide variety in sentence structure.

When sharing a book with your child, read in short stretches, pausing often to talk about the pictures. Have your child turn the pages and point to the pictures and familiar words. And be sure to reread favorite stories or parts of stories.

There is no right or wrong way to share books with children. Find time to read with your child and pass on the legacy of literacy.

Adria F. Klein, Ph.D.
Professor Emeritus
California State University
San Bernardino, California

First American edition published in 2003 by
Picture Window Books
5115 Excelsior Boulevard
Suite 232
Minneapolis, MN 55416
1-877-845-8392
www.picturewindowbooks.com

First published in Great Britain by Franklin Watts, 96 Leonard Street, London, EC2A 4XD
Text © Jillian Powell 2000
Illustration © Amanda Wood 2000

Printed in the United States of America.
1 2 3 4 5 6 08 07 06 05 04 03

Library of Congress Cataloging-in-Publication Data
Powell, Jillian.
  Recycled! / written by Jillian Powell ; illustrated by Amanda Wood.—1st American ed.
    p. cm. — (Read-it! readers)
  Summary: Miss Drew's efforts to teach her class about recycling are very successful.
  ISBN 1-4048-0068-9
  [1. Recycling (Waste)—Fiction. 2. Schools—Fiction.] I. Wood, Amanda, ill. II. Title. III. Series.
  PZ7.P87755 Re 2003
  [E]—dc21   2002074807

Recycled!

Written by Jillian Powell

Illustrated by Amanda Wood

Reading Advisors:
Adria F. Klein, Ph.D.
Professor Emeritus, California State University
San Bernardino, California

Ruth Thomas
Durham Public Schools
Durham, North Carolina

R. Ernice Bookout
Durham Public Schools
Durham, North Carolina

Picture Window Books
Minneapolis, Minnesota

Miss Drew's class was
learning about recycling.

"Let's start a recycling bin," said Miss Drew.

"We can put it out in the hall."

Some people brought bottles.
Some people brought cans.

Others brought newspapers,
egg cartons, or old clothes.

Soon, the recycling bin
was almost full.

"Next week, we'll take it to the recycling center in town," said Miss Drew.

Miss Han was the art
teacher.

She looked in the bin and saw all the egg cartons.

"We'll use them to make an
alligator," she told Miss Drew.

So she took them back to her classroom.

Mrs. Bell, the lunchroom lady, saw all the bottles and jars.

"I'll use these for my jam,"
she told Miss Drew.

So, she took them home
and made lots of jam.

Strawberry
Jam

19

Mr. Timms, the principal,
was moving.

He needed something to wrap his dishes in.

"These newspapers are just what I need," he told Miss Drew.

So he used them to wrap
up his dishes.

Mr. Green, the custodian,
saw the tin cans.

"I know what I can do with these," he told Miss Drew.

Mrs. Roberts, the gym teacher, saw the old woolen clothes.

"These are just what I need,"
she told Miss Drew.

When the class came to get the recycling bin, it was empty.

"It's all been recycled!" said Miss Drew.

So they started recycling
all over again!

Red Level

The Best Snowman, by Margaret Nash 1-4048-0048-4
Bill's Baggy Pants, by Susan Gates 1-4048-0050-6
Cleo and Leo, by Anne Cassidy 1-4048-0049-2
Felix on the Move, by Maeve Friel 1-4048-0055-7
Jasper and Jess, by Anne Cassidy 1-4048-0061-1
The Lazy Scarecrow, by Jillian Powell 1-4048-0062-X
Little Joe's Big Race, by Andy Blackford 1-4048-0063-8
The Little Star, by Deborah Nash 1-4048-0065-4
The Naughty Puppy, by Jillian Powell 1-4048-0067-0
Selfish Sophie, by Damian Kelleher 1-4048-0069-7

Blue Level

The Bossy Rooster, by Margaret Nash 1-4048-0051-4
Jack's Party, by Ann Bryant 1-4048-0060-3
Little Red Riding Hood, by Maggie Moore 1-4048-0064-6
Recycled!, by Jillian Powell 1-4048-0068-9
The Sassy Monkey, by Anne Cassidy 1-4048-0058-1
The Three Little Pigs, by Maggie Moore 1-4048-0071-9

Yellow Level

Cinderella, by Barrie Wade 1-4048-0052-2
The Crying Princess, by Anne Cassidy 1-4048-0053-0
Eight Enormous Elephants, by Penny Dolan 1-4048-0054-9
Freddie's Fears, by Hilary Robinson 1-4048-0056-5
Goldilocks and the Three Bears, by Barrie Wade 1-4048-0057-3
Mary and the Fairy, by Penny Dolan 1-4048-0066-2
Jack and the Beanstalk, by Maggie Moore 1-4048-0059-X
The Three Billy Goats Gruff, by Barrie Wade 1-4048-0070-0